The Treasure
of the Muleteer

The Treasure
of the Muleteer

AND OTHER

SPANISH TALES

Told by Antonio Jiménez-Landi

Translated from the Spanish by Paul Blackburn

Illustrated by Floyd Sowell

Doubleday & Company, Inc./Garden City, New York

ISBN: 0-385-08027-1 Trade
       0-385-07041-1 Prebound
Library of Congress Catalog Card Number 73–11698
Translation and Illustrations Copyright © 1974 by Doubleday & Company, Inc.

Preface

SPAIN, A COUNTRY AS VARIED in its geography as its history is
old, has a handsome treasure in its legends. Some come down
from ancient times, themes which run throughout the medi-
eval world. One would have to be very bold to try to identify
their origins. Others were inspired by local myths deriving
from a pre-Christian epoch, and which still persist in the
superstitions of the people. Finally, many exist which derive
from anonymous poems based, in turn, on some historical occurrence, more or less exaggerated by popular inspiration.

Very characteristic of our native narratives are their links to
the great undertaking of the Reconquest, and therefore the pro-
tagonists of these tales may be, and frequently are, Moorish.
The Moors are often given magical qualities, a result, no
doubt, of the prestige attained by Muslim physicians and
astronomers during the brilliant epoch of the Caliphate at
Córdoba, even under the corrupt kingdoms of the Taifas
after the Caliphate at Córdoba had broken up.

In the present book, I have tried to select one legend
characteristic of each of the great regions into which the
Spanish portion of the Iberian Peninsula is historically divided.
With these, the readers may catch a glimpse of how much remains unsaid.

—ANTONIO JIMÉNEZ-LANDI

Contents

The Treasure
of the Muleteer

CASTILE

The Legend of
Fernán González

IT WAS DURING THE YEARS when the caliphs of Córdoba dominated nearly all of Spain. The Christian princes to the north
fought resolutely to maintain their small kingdoms against the
Muslim power, but were hardly more than hanging by their
fingernails from the rocks of the Pyrenees and the Cantabrian
Mountains, back above the Ebro and the Duero, the great
rivers that acted as their natural defense.

The Muslims gave little heed to these northern kingdoms,
which they could have destroyed easily—a lion killing a fly
with a single thud of the paw; but the fly never left off biting
the lion every chance it got, and there were a number of
propitious occasions. Generally, during the summer, it was
usual that a more or less fair-sized body of troops would in-
vade Muslim territory to seize some frontier castle and destroy the crops just as the harvest was about to begin, while
at the same time the caliph's army was busy immolating the
Christians' farmlands or taking one of their fortresses by assault.

This backing and forthing was usual in such a drawn-out
conflict, which had lasted since Tarik's and Muza's troops had
invaded Spanish territory, and Pelayo, the valiant Christian
chieftain, had faced about and offered resistance on the craggy
brushwood tangles of Covadonga.

At this point in time, the caliph Hisen II, son and heir of the great Alhaken of the glorious reign, was ruler in renowned Córdoba, the large city on the Guadalquivir. But the man who really ruled, the true lord of Al-Andalus (in Arabic that means Spain), was his general and first minister, Almanzor, a name which still means *the Victorious*.

The campaigns of this chieftain, prodigious because of his political talent, his endowments as a great warrior, and his sizable ambition, had laid an enforced peace, more like death than anything else, upon the kings of León and Asturias, of Aragón and Navarre. Not one of these princes dared attack the invincible Muslim, governor of Córdoba who, in the full climax of his aggressions, had destroyed León completely, leaving, however, a single of its towers standing, that it might serve as a monument to his victory. At a different time, he had marched as far as the venerated sepulcher of the apostle Santiago in Galicia. After profaning the shrine and sacking it, he tore down the sonorous bells which had tolled so long and beautifully over the green, melancholy valleys of Compostela. Loading them onto the backs of Christian captives, Almanzor had them carted all the way down to Córdoba where, in the famous mezquita (mosque) there, he offered them to Allah.

So, during these unhappy years for the servitors of Christ, in the county of Castile, a small district in the far eastern part of the kingdom of León, there governed a restless lord who was called Fernán González.

Like other knights of his time, Fernán González was very fond of hunting. Handling weapons was his principal business, so that when he was not using them to fend off Moors or in other exercises suitable to knighthood, he devoted their use to big-game hunting. Game was quite abundant in the mountains and valleys which surrounded the town of Lara, located on the banks of a small stream that emptied its waters into the Arlanza, between Salas and Covarrubias.

One day when Fernán González was riding out to hunt among these mountains covered with brakes and thickets, a wild boar rushed out of a clump of underbrush. The beast was magnificent, and the count began the chase, jumping his horse over endless thickets and rough terrain with not a thing on his mind but to take him.

The pig always escaped him, but never got completely out of sight, nor put himself in position for an easy kill, so that Fernán González did not decide to abandon the quarry, nor could he get at it, much less take it. The hunter and the animal, one right behind the other, raced down almost to the banks of the Arlanza, which, in that part of its course, ran between pinewoods and thickets. The boar scuttered with agility between the thicket clumps, and the count's horse galloped just behind . . . until, just on the point of overtaking him, the horse's hoofs and shanks got trapped, tangled in the thick underbrush—he couldn't budge. The count leaped to the ground and drew his sword to kill the boar, but at that moment the animal raced to a hermit's cave half hidden in the growth and went right inside it. And once inside, he sought refuge behind the altar.

The good count also bent down and entered the tiny shrine; but respecting the sacred enclosure, instead of wounding the boar, he knelt in front of the altar to offer a prayer.

He'd hardly begun when a monk came out of the sacristy. A very old man with a very long beard, his feet were bare and he supported himself on a knotty, twisted staff.

"Be welcome and come in peace, good count, and now that the pursuit of a boar has led you to this holy place, you must know that it's time to give up hunting animals, and that you are going to meet in combat Almanzor, the scourge of Christianity. A tough battle is waiting for you, because the enemy army is very numerous and very strong; but you shall gain great renown in that fight. Before the start of that combat, you must see a token, a sign that'll make your beard shake and terrorize your knights. See to the battle then, which you will win, and afterward take as wife a good lady whose name is Doña Sancha. You will undergo great afflictions, then, twice, you will find yourself shut in a dark prison, shackled and constrained by bars, but your glory will be very high, and if one day you reach honor and power, you will not forget this lowly hermitage lost amid the mountains."

Fernán González ended up puzzled but grateful. He said good-by to the elderly monk, mounted his horse, and went to meet his men who, impatient, were already searching for him among the thick groves of oak.

II

Almanzor came, in fact, riding across the whole of the land of Castile with a powerful army: he laid waste to mountains, he set grainfields on fire, destroyed farmhouses, stormed towns . . .

Fernán González got his armed retinue together and sallied out to meet him. They saw already in the distance the innumerable forces of the governor of Córdoba. The Castilian made a quick recount of the pennons with him and figured that they were very few to go into combat with the Mohammedans who were advancing across the countryside like the waves of a storm at sea.

While the count was considering the most viable solution to the problem, one of the knights broke ranks and, galloping hard, got a good distance forward of the small army . . . At which point the earth opened just in front of his mount, beast and rider disappeared down the great cleft, which snapped back then and closed over them.

The count and his men felt a profound terror; a fearful dread raised the hair on the heads of men well-accustomed to the horrors of war.

But immediately, Fernán González was hugely elated.

Wasn't this the sign the hermit had predicted? And reining his charger to face the troops, cried:

"Knights! Nothing to fear! What you've just seen is the signal of our victory, for if the earth itself is incapable of resisting us, how can the might of the infidels prevail against us? Santiago! Charge!"

See the lances set in their sockets, shields up covering the chests, pennons fluttering at the fore of those filled squadrons of horsemen . . . and a hundred, a thousand, two thousand coursers at full gallop against the caliph's soldiers who were moving forward in closed ranks, preceded by the great, throbbing drums.

The distance lessens between the two armies. Every minute the faces of the enemy grow larger and the peril stands closer . . . Santiago! Close it up! Now!!!

And the sharp lances and terrible pikes drove the first Mohammedan riders out of their saddles. Cleft helmets, chilabas (hooded garments), and coats of mail torn to shreds, leather shields pierced through, broken lances and shattered swords were strewn all over the field. The finest Andalusian horses poured their blood out upon the ground . . .

"Santiago!! Charge!!!"

By the end of the afternoon, the field was covered with corpses and wounded men lying among the spoils of the battle. Those Moors who survived were in flight, sheltered by the shadows of nightfall. Fernán González has conquered; the booty he recovers is immense . . . Thanks be to the Lord who has protected the valiant Castilians.

The count then sets aside a portion of the unbelievably rich booty, and with it starts out for the banks of the Arlanza River. He passes into the hermit's cave and hands the good monk wealth considerable enough to build a church to the Lord.

Still today, the ruins of the famous monastery of San Pedro de Arlanza, its crumbled ogive arches and collapsed walls

above the stones of a primitive Romanesque temple, attest to the truth of this famous legend.

III

CASTILE WAS A DISTRICT UNDER TRIBUTE to the kingdom of León, whose sovereign appointed the counts who had then to govern it.

At that time, king Don Sancho wished to convene the Cortes (Court), and sent a message to advise Fernán González that he should attend. The Castilian was highly reluctant to go, as he did not wish to kiss the king of León's hand. Castile wanted its independence, and its good count refused to bend his knee before the king.

For exactly this reason, furthermore, the monarch rode out to welcome Fernán González in an attempt to cajole him, to offer him greater honors, so as, in this way, to lure him more easily.

The count carried on his wrist a handsome goshawk and was riding a magnificent courser he'd won in the battle against the terrible Almanzor.

"You reckon on having a good horse there, Count," the king said, "even your hawk makes me jealous. I'd be much obliged if you'd sell me both animals."

"The lord need not pay for what his vassal owns. In any case, they're yours," answered Fernán González.

But the king did not want to take them for nothing and started to insist that they should be purchased, that he would not have them at all if he could not buy them.

Fernán González set a price then for the hawk and the charger, a price that seemed very low to the sovereign.

"My lord, as you have insisted upon paying, I've sold you my goshawk and my horse at a price I consider fair; all right, I'll add one condition: between the delivery of the goods and the day when you pay me their value, each day that goes by their price will double."

"Agreed," said the king.

He took Fernán González's horse and the hawk . . . and immediately forgot the deal he'd made with the count.

Seven years passed . . . at the end of which time, the king of León summoned the Cortes again, and again called on the count of Castile to attend it. But the count, instead of hurrying up to León, let two more years go by.

The monarch, extremely annoyed at his vassal's conduct, and furthermore, it had been a long time since he'd paid the tribute he owed, writing again to the count, threatened to take away his position and title, and to banish him from Castile.

Fernán González, then, went up to León. The king had already arrived there. Fernán presented himself before Don Sancho, planted one knee on the ground and asked for the monarch's hand to kiss.

But the king denied him, and giving way to his suppressed rage, called him unfaithful and a traitor, before the whole Court.

Fernán González regained his feet and spoke: "Milord, nine years ago when I came to the Cortes, I sold you my horse and my hawk; furthermore, up till now, today, you haven't paid me their price. Make up the bill that you owe me, and I'll refund the difference, if there be any."

The arrogance of Fernán González upset Don Sancho even more. He ordered the count immediately seized and put in a gloomy dungeon, set in chains, and fastened in firmly with heavy bars.

The news of this calamity reached the ears of the countess, Doña Sancha, who, without losing time, set out on the road to León with a troop of three hundred Castilians of noble descent. But Doña Sancha's impatience to see her husband was so great that she rode far to the fore of everyone, and soon found herself alone at the feet of the king. She begged his permission to see the prisoner, and was immediately conducted to the tower where he resided.

Doña Sancha, addressing herself to the count then, said to him:

"Quickly, milord, get up and change clothes with me."

And in the bat of an eyelash the exchange was made. Shortly thereafter, then, someone in women's clothes disappeared out the gate where the countess had entered, and some other person, in prisoner's garb, stayed in the tower.

The following day, however, the ladies and three hundred noblemen who had come with Doña Sancha entered León and presented themselves before the king, demanding their lady's liberty.

"What lady?" answered the sovereign.

"Our countess, Doña Sancha, whom you have imprisoned with no reason whatever for doing so."

The king begged their pardon and ordered that the jail be opened so that the Castilians would be convinced of their mistake. But, upon entering the cell, everyone saw to his astonishment that, in actuality, the prisoner was not the count, but his wife.

Don Sancho wished to take no reprisals, inasmuch as Fernán González was still in his lands, and any action he might have taken against his wife had to be avenged, ferociously, by the most dreaded warrior in his kingdom. So, then, he released the captive, even had her escorted by a splendid guard of honor.

Once freed (count and countess both), Fernán González demanded of the king that he pay the price agreed for the hawk and the horse.

But when the king and his councilors counted up the price, doubling the initial price for every day that had passed since the date of purchase, they saw there was not enough money in the kingdom of León to pay the debt.

So, then, it proved more economical to cancel the taxes for which the count was indebted to the king, and to include, furthermore, any tribute he would owe from that time forward.

In this way, Fernán González ended by securing the independence of Castile, for the price of a horse and a goshawk.

GALICIA

The Treasure of
the Muleteer

IT'S ALWAYS BEEN SAID that women have a propensity for being overcurious, and that, on occasions, this unwholesome curiosity visits severe annoyances upon them and their husbands. And if not, what else might he say, that muleteer from Sobrado del Obispo who lost a fortune through his wife's being curious—curious and gossipy—another sin that afflicts many housewives.

It so happens that Galicia, that beautiful land, is inhabited by Galicians and by Moors. Everyone sees the Galicians, but the Moors . . . only the Galicians see them. Nonetheless, these Moors have done and are still doing great things. One of their constructions are castros, those concentric circles of rough boulders situated on nearly inaccessible hilltops, and which archaeologists attributed to primitive men. Because modern sages, in the vanity of their sciences, do not believe that there can still be charmed beings who live under the earth and are invisible.

One who really believed in them, though, was a muleteer of Sobrado del Obispo who carted wine to the outlying villages in his ponderous, creaking cart. He wore out the tracks of the road between his village and Orense, carrying wineskins filled with a rich vintage to his customers of that city, which was the seat of the bishopric. And among his customers, believe it or not, the most important ones were the Moors.

From time to time, our man went to a wine vault, filled his wineskins with the best small wine of Ribeiro, and started down the road to Orense, humming to himself.

Once in the city, he'd climb with his span of mules up to the Castros de Trelles, two outcroppings that shut off a view of the town all the way to the Portuguese frontier. The apparition of the Moors, the ancient founders of the castros, waited for him there. They came up from underground where they occupied the interminable corridors and passages with which they had mined the entire region. These passages relied upon only two entrances, one to the east and the other to the west. The Moors swarmed up from out of one of them, loaded up the wine the muleteer had just brought them, and in payment placed into his eager hands small fragments of shale extracted from the depths of the earth.

The muleteer stored the small hunks of gray rock in his pouch, and when he arrived back home and emptied the purse, the chips of slate had transformed themselves into gold pieces.

The muleteer's trips to the Castros de Trelles were frequently repeated. He went down every day finally, and as a consequence, the good man's fortune was growing continually, which pleased him no end.

His wife, who was very nosy, began to carp at the strange phenomenon. Not too far back, for instance, he could barely dispose of his merchandise after traveling all over the territory, and now, every single day, he came back with his purse full of gold pieces.

As was logical, the good wife asked her husband the source of all that so-easily-earned money.

But the muleteer from Sobrado was unable to answer, as the Moors had obliged him to swear that he would tell no one the sort of clients he had. So the man either kept his mouth shut, or made some excuse or another to change the subject of conversation.

"Aren't you satisfied with the pig and the heifer you bought at the market in Barbantes? What's the difference to you how I earn the money?"

But the good wife insisted, again and again.

"You must tell me about it, lovey, you've got to tell me; men shouldn't have secrets from their wives."

And morning, noon, afternoon, and night . . . every hour on the hour, constantly, constantly:

"You have to tell me, lovey . . ."

The man couldn't stay in his house a single second without hearing the same old song . . .

And he thought that, one of the two: either he left his hearth forever, or he revealed the Moors' secret to his wife.

In a moment of weakness he chose the latter course; but, oh yes, certainly, with all kinds of precautions. When everyone in the village was asleep, and you couldn't hear anything but the thin, mewling cry of the heifer from the stable redolent with hay smell, the muleteer led his good wife to the farthest corner of the house and there told her what was happening. But careful! Be sure you tell no one! Not even the Moors, who know everything, must know that I've told you this.

The idea! What nonsense, as discreet and quiet as she was? They'd have to get the penedos (isolated rocky peaks) of the Monte *das* Cantariñas to talk, or the stone angels on the doorway of the church of the Gloria, before they'd get the Moors' secret from her . . .

And the following morning, when the good muleteer had loaded his wagon and left for the Castros de Trelles, his good wife meddled over to Mariquiña's house and began to whisper . . . and left Mariquiña's and sat herself down in Carmiña's stable and went on whispering, and went from Carmiña's stable to the Carboeira grocery store, leaned on her elbows there and chattered some more . . .

"Do you know my husband is the one that drives wine

to the Moors? But, shhh! don't go and tell anyone, not anyone . . ."

Mariquiña, and Carmiña, and la Carboeira, when they saw
their respective husbands, they scolded them:

"How does that look! You spend every day working, sunup
to sundown to earn four coppers that won't last you till nightfall, and the muleteer makes one easy trip to carry wine and
comes back with a pocketful of gold. You could do what he
does . . . Sell something to the Moors . . . Yes, yes, to the
Moors . . ."

The muleteer arrived at the Castros de Trelles that day,
his leather wineskins bursting with good Ribeiro. But he
waited in vain for the mysterious buyers to make themselves
visible. No one showed up. The eastern entrance and the
western entrance, both stayed shut tight.

The muleteer returned home as though nothing had happened—the Gallegos are tough when luck turns her face
away from them—and the neighbors in Sobrado del Obispo
were peeking out of their windows to see him pass. He passed
with his face grim, and I have a mind to say that he was
muttering between his teeth. His good wife came out to greet
him:

"You know? I didn't say anything to anyone, not to anyone . . ."

The muleteer also said nothing. He rolled up his sleeves on
those sturdy arms that could hold down an ox by the nape
of its neck, and Zas! Zas! he whupped his wife until he got
tired of beating her.

But the luck had left them, and for good.

ASTURIAS

The Xana Spring

THE MUSLIMS WERE WINDING UP THE CONQUEST of the Iberian Peninsula, from the headland of Tarifa to the Cantabrian Mountains, where the noble Visigoth, Pelayo, and a few but valiant Christians had finally halted the infidels' offensive. This Christian nucleus was the origin of the tiny kingdom of Asturias that had its capital at Cangas de Onís. But beyond the valleys of the Sella River and the Nalón, the whole rest of the territory on the peninsula was under Moorish power; consequently, no prince was so bold as to deny the emirs or their military chiefs anything that they might ask.

For the most part, the Muslim generals came from North Africa, and held the white-skinned blondes of the Asturian region in high esteem. So, then, taking advantage of their unchallenged power and of the weakness and indolence of the Asturian king, Mauregato, they imposed a shameful tribute, which consisted of delivering a hundred maidens every year for the pleasure of the emir of the true believers of Islam, who governed from Córdoba.

This happened in about the last decade of the eighth century, only twenty years after the crushing defeat of the king, Don Rodrigo, on the banks of the Guadalete.

As an additional humiliation, the king of Asturias himself was appointed as the agent to choose the hundred maidens and to deliver them to the Muslim troops. But, not content with his despicable charge, he always chose those who were among the loveliest, so as to keep his enemies very happy, and so as not to disturb his peaceful and leisurely life.

As the date of the cruel surrender approached, Mauregato's soldiers—who had never had to fight against the infidels— scoured the small villages of the kingdom and seized the hundred girls by main force, taking the most beautiful maidens, so as to deliver them to the Moors. These unhappy damsels would never again see their fathers or brothers, friends or neighbors. In some Godforsaken spot in the vastness of Andalucia, they would fade away forlorn next to a Mohammedan husband who would have obliged them to change their religion.

The tribute of a hundred maidens: it was cruel, inhuman, intolerable; but no one would venture to rebel against it, fearing Mauregato's anger, for it was in this way that he bought peace on his frontiers.

At the entrance to Avilés lived a couple with a daughter called Galinda, and so lovely that she could not be matched by anyone in the region.

As the girl grew older, she grew even more beautiful, and her parents watched the process with growing terror since they figured the day would arrive when the king's soldiers would be passing through the village . . . which happened, finally. An evil day. They knocked heavily on the door of the house. Unprepared, the mother went to open the door, and saw in the shadowed doorway the beaky faces of the soldiers and their weapons. She was terrified.

The poor mother stood there as though she'd been struck dead. But just then she remembered, her daughter had gone to fetch water.

The warriors did not state the purpose which had led them there. They confined themselves to asking for lodging for the night; then—according to them—they were proceeding elsewhere, another sector of the country, where the monarch had entrusted them with a particular commission.

And at that moment, not suspecting the kind of people then inside the modest abode, here we have Galinda, who comes in the door, singing as always.

She was not that slow that the soldiers' real intention escaped her; but she hid her fear and started to sing some very lovely Asturian melodies, accompanying herself with dancing, with the result that those hardened men were delighted, watching and listening to the precious girl.

But Galinda was very bright, and she realized that, as soon as the songs and dancing were over, the warriors of Mauregato would seize her and hand her over to the Moors with ninety-nine other luckless girls. So she suggested to the crew of soldiers that she sing a song and dance a dance even more beautiful than the ones they had been admiring, but that you could only do it out in the fields and under moonlight.

The king's soldiers accepted the idea with great merriment, and all went out into the meadow that surrounded the small house.

Once they were outside, Galinda began to put some distance between her and the group of men, under the pretext of seeking a site more suitable for the mysterious dance. And when she figured she was sufficiently far away from her would-be abductors, she began racing across the mountainside so swiftly that those deluded warriors could not catch up. But her endurance was coming to an end and it was necessary to find someplace to hide herself before that happened. So, then, Galinda arrived at the spring falling from the high rock, intending to hide herself behind it. But as she came closer, she heard a melodious voice, that had to be the water's voice, which said to her:

"Should you like to be my xana, the days of your life will pass happily."

(As the oldest of Asturian myths tell it, a xana was a species of nymph or caryatid.)

"And what must I do to change me into a xana?" asked Galinda.

"Take a sip of my water, then you will not only find your-self free of the king's soldiers, but you will have ended for-ever the tribute of the hundred maidens."

The girl grew very happy to hear such words which gushed forth from the spring itself; she knelt down before it and, with faith and anxiety together, drank a sip of water, and at the same instant saw the surface of the falling water open to hide her in its depths.

The whole mountain resounded with the soldiers' voices:

"Galinda! Galindaaa!"

But in the ravines and valleys, only the echo answered, re-peating:

"Galindaaa!"

The young girl had disappeared as if by enchantment. Night had fallen already, and it was useless to continue the search.

The soldiers returned to her parents' house, spent the night there, and the following morning, at the first whiteness of dawn, they flung out across the countryside again to run down the girl who had made them a laughing stock. You can imagine how furiously they stalked her. And! if they ever found her . . .

While floundering about, they came to a clear fount, and coming closer, heard a soft and marvelous music. Surprised, the soldiers hid themselves to observe whoever it was who was singing so tenderly . . . And they saw a very lovely creature, luminous and glittering, resembling very much the lass they had come seeking. Yes, it was she, no doubt about it; but even more lovely and enchanting than the evening before. She was under the waterfall, combing her long, blond hair with a small golden comb, all the while she was singing, de-lighting them with her voice which seemed supernatural at this point.

The soldiers hesitated; but finally they advanced toward her . . .

Galinda, who was already the xana of the spring, fixed her

eyes, green as the water was, upon the soldiers, and instantly the fierce warriors were transformed into curly haired, woolly sheep.

Time went by, and Mauregato was in a magnificent temper because the day when he was to deliver the hundred maidens was approaching quickly, and his troops had not returned.

Inasmuch as they were late, he sent out another group, even more numerous, and, if anything, soldiers more savage than the first ones. The small squadron of soldiers followed the same roads as the first troop, but without finding a trace of them anywhere in the district.

Following directions, given them by some villagers they'd met, they found themselves on the road to Illés—that was the name of Avilés in such remote times. And there the information led them to believe that the earlier group of soldiers had marched to a certain mountainous area where there was a spring of water . . .

The soldiers closed in on the point indicated, when an astonishing voice filled them with terror.

Not far off, a young woman of supernatural beauty was spinning wool at the edge of a spring while a flock of robust, white sheep were feeding in the pasture about her.

The silky wool that the young shepherdess was weaving on her wheel and bobbin doubtless came from these frizzled fleeces . . . The warriors advanced slowly, as though drawn by the astonishing vision. The xana's glance fell upon them and, upon the instant, they also were transformed into sheep.

And the days passed, and the weeks, and already it was more than enough time that the troop sent out behind the first should have returned to Pravia, where Mauregato was with his army.

But no one, absolutely no one, could give the king the slightest news about what had happened to his soldiers. They had been seen entering Avilés, but no one had seen them leave.

His turn come round at last, Mauregato gathered together the choicest of his host, the most valorous knights, the toughest veterans among his foot soldiers, rode off and set his army before the town that he believed was both rebel and traitorous, and was ready to pass every one of its inhabitants under the knife, to tear down their tiny houses and seed the countryside with salt. He was set in his mind that the men of war that he'd sent out earlier had to show up safe and sound.

But no one knew anything in Avilés, except that two batches of troops had penetrated the country into the mountains, following a road that ended at a spring . . .

And the king commanded his men:

"Follow me . . ."

And he headed toward the Xana spring.

It was a cold spring in the middle of a green pasture, ringed about with thick chestnut trees and oaks.

A very lovely maiden was stretching out white skeins of wool upon the tender grasses to dry in the sun, and, what seemed likely enough, the sheep of an already numerous flock were grazing peacefully.

The king spurred his horse forward, and when the damsel raised her eyes, green as the grass where she walked, and clear as the water of the spring, the monarch was already upon her.

"Xana," Mauregato demanded, "where are my soldiers? Come, answer me."

"What soldiers, milord?" Galinda asked.

"The ones I sent to collect the hundred maidens."

"The ones you sent, milord, were not soldiers, they were sheep."

"What? You dare laugh at the king? They were soldiers, the same as those who follow me here now."

"The soldiers who follow you, milord, are also sheep, and you indeed might be their shepherd," answered Galinda with great civility.

The king turned around. His troops had disappeared in

some mysterious manner, and in their place he saw a flock of sheep, even larger than the one which surrounded the Xana.

Instinctively, Mauregato looked down at himself, and astonished, saw that he had lost his horse, that his coat of mail, his helmet, and his arms had changed themselves into the coarse, sheepskin jacket an apprentice shepherd of the district might wear, fitted out with a leather gamebag and a shepherd's crook like any mountain sheepherder. His hands were rough and wrinkled, and his face tanned and weatherbeaten by the sun.

He was terrified, but overcoming the fear that silenced him, he addressed the lovely maiden begging her that she work the enchantment off all of them.

"And whatever more you want, Xana," the king begged her, "return me my horse and arms, and my regal face . . . turn those lambs back into my soldiers again and I'll grant whatever you ask of me . . ."

"The issue is in your hands," Galinda replied. "Break that criminal treaty of the hundred maidens, or should you decide not to, you will neither recover your face, nor will the sheep turn back into soldiers; quite the contrary, all the soldiers that come to look for you will meet the same fate as these."

Mauregato figured correctly that there was no other alternative than to concede to Galinda's most pressing demands; he said:

"I promise you under the king's oath." Immediately the sheep resumed their figuration as men; the helmet, cuirass, and the arms covered the sovereign's body once more.

The Xana had disappeared, and the king returned to Pravia, surrounded by his mighty host.

From Pravia, Mauregato sent letters to the emir of Córdoba letting him know that, from henceforward, it would be impossible to complete the terms of the agreement, because it was opposed by a mysterious creature, against whose will he could not fight.

Thanks to the lovely and intelligent Galinda, the humiliating and cruel tribute had ended forever.

In Avilés, the Xana Spring still exists. Let it serve as my witness.

BASQUE COUNTRY

Ari Biyur

THERE'S A SHRINE over near Oyarzun where Santiago and San Felipe are worshiped; furthermore, in the times of Maricastaña, the place was consecrated to Our Lady.

On one occasion, a French woman of high lineage, very beautiful and capricious, had just crossed the frontier, and was passing the small temple.

The haughty lady was escorted by a cortége, if not brilliant, at least very splendid indeed, which was commanded by an elegant knight who rode at her side.

The lovely lady, with great elegance and agility was mounted on a courser of prime quality, and the knight on a mettlesome sorrel. Lady and knight approached, conversing in a lively fashion; the young man flirting with the lady, and the lady allowing herself to be flirted with.

In this way they arrived at Oyarzun, and while resting to regain their strength a bit, out of curiosity they entered the modest hermitage.

The lady was a person of little faith; she took in the poor enclosure at a glance, and finally her eyes came to rest on the statue of Our Lady. Her gallant fell to his knees and prayed from down there, not presuming further.

All of a sudden, the elegant horsewoman's glance fell upon an exquisite rosary between Our Lady's fingers, and said to her pious companion:

"What a wonder! A gem without equal! Would you dare to hand me that rosary?"

The knight tried to dissuade her.

"If it were not in the hand of Our Lady," he answered courteously, "I confess that no other hand would better deserve it than yours."

"As long as you feel that way about it, and the Lady who has it is no more than a statue, you should have no objection to handing it to me."

"Sacred objects, lady, ought to remain where they are, for he who made them set them there . . ."

"All right, I'm telling you that I want that rosary and that I have to have it, for I've never seen one like it. Nor will you deny that no wooden sculpture can enjoy it the way I would enjoy it."

"It would be easy for you to find an artist who would make another even more exquisite and more beautiful."

"As for me, I happen to very much fancy that one."

"Who knows, it might have been the votive offering of a sick person who recovered his health through the mediation of the Sainted Virgin, or some mother, or grateful wife . . ."

"Bah! That's outright foolishness. And it's a shame that such a gem is there, in this poor shrine, where no one can look at it or value it. If you'll not dare give it to me, you'll see right soon that I'll reach for it myself."

Said and done; the lady climbed the altar and undid the rosary from the virgin's hand. Then she studied it between her fingers merrily, and put it carefully into her purse.

No one had seen the theft. The lady walked out of the shrine smiling, and her young companion followed her, not daring to raise his eyes to the despoiled statue.

With agility and grace, the lady mounted her horse, the young man vaulted onto his own, and the small cortège started moving again.

From time to time, she glanced wantonly at the knight, as though wanting him to be a partner to her secret. The

knight reproached himself inwardly for his lack of valor in having consented to the sacrilegious theft . . . and the light-hearted and cheerful conversation did not resume. Then the lady assumed the haughty attitude which had not left her . . .

Coming from the opposite direction along the road was a bedraggled little old man, dressed very poorly, who, upon arriving before the lady and her retinue, cried out in a deep, ponderous voice:

"Travelers, halt!"

In spite of the fact that the figure of the old man could hardly inspire anyone with terror, his posture inspired respect, and several men in the escort laid hands to their swords.

The old man, in a thunderous voice which did not alter, said:

"No one need fear, solely the person who has something to fear. Of the rest of you I ask nothing."

And then, turning to the lady, he added:

"Just you, I ask that you return the rosary you have just stolen from the Holy Virgin at the shrine."

The lady grew pale, more from anger than from fear, but she managed to restrain herself and denied it scornfully.

"What does the man say? I've not robbed anyone. This old man is out of his head and doesn't know what he's saying."

But the white-haired, little old man replied:

"I know that you are she who, under an evil temptation, has just taken the Virgin's rosary with your own hands . . ."

And the lady, beside herself in an excess of rage, shouted:

"Ari biyur! (May I be turned to stone) if what I say is not true."

And instantly, the lady turned into a rock.

You can still, today, see a boulder in the shape of a woman on horseback, near the shrine.

ARAGÓN

The Legend of
San Juan de Atarés

IN THE YEAR 711 of our era, the Muslims of Mauretania set foot on the Iberian Peninsula, summoned by the sons of King Witiza to help them attain the throne occupied at that moment by Roderico or Rodrigo.

Tarik commanded the force, defeated Roderico on the banks of the Guadalete or the Barbate, and continued the conquest of the country up to Toledo, the Visigoth capital. There he joined forces with Muza, the governor of Mauretania, who had also crossed the Straits of Gibraltar, attracted, no doubt, by the news continually arriving about the victorious expedition of his subordinate. And while the latter continued his advance into other parts of Spanish territory, Muza led his army against the important city of Caesaraugusta, which later came to be called Zaragoza.

Before the sweeping power of the invaders, the terrified natives fled, hiding themselves in the rough crags of the Pyrenees. Among the mountains they began to build small towns where they lived with what was left of their household possessions.

The fugitives occupied the banks of the Gállego and Aragón rivers which fall down through the valley of Canfranc, whose towering summit can be seen from far off. The landscape is grandiose. The barricade of the Pyrenees rises like a curtain in the background, massive and white above the deserted plain, which the river, very blue, cuts through.

La Maladeta, Posets, El Vignemale, the Pic du Midi, are ten thousand feet up, and dominate even the summit of Monte Perdido.

An icy wind blows, and the sun barely heats the ground where a standing wall of rock hides it with its huge, violet presence.

In the shelter of Pano Mountain you could see a fortress; its builders had called it by the same name as the mountain, and around about were a series of sheds under which the future inhabitants of the town-under-construction dwelt. In this barren spot lived an old man with a beard as venerable as the Pyrenees, as white and as long as its rivers.

Now this old man had two sons, Félix and Oto, young men, both of whom also worked at building the village. Every day the father went out to cut trees in the pine and oak groves nearby.

But one evening, back from his hard toil, he sits down before his fire, his head sunken and gloomy. His sons notice his deep preoccupation, and after exchanging understanding glances, they ask him the reason for his low spirits.

"My sons: I'm sure the infidels will fall upon Pano and demolish it, just as they've done with so many other villages."

"Why do you think so, Father?"

"Because, just this afternoon, I was on my way back from logging and heard a cry of pain, a moan almost. I stopped, noted it, and the cry came again, at the same time a depressing melody filled the valleys."

The sons remained silent. The old man continued:

"I suspect you've guessed it . . . Oh yes, my sons: it was the song of the Maladeta, sounds like a woman weeping; a melancholy voice that issues from the accursed rock every time some great disaster is about to happen."

There was an oppressive silence.

"Keep talking, Father," the young men said, finally.

"Then I'd hardly turned down the trail, when I saw that the Cúculo peak was covered by black clouds, terrible and threatening . . ."

These two signs were deadly, and the three men threw themselves to their knees and began to pray.

Enormous bonfires clustered around the builders of the town and their families. Night had fallen and everyone had retired. The moon was beginning to rise in the dark sky, and the valleys were lit up by its icy brightness.

Then the old man called his son Oto, and asked that he climb with him to the highest tower of the fortress, for it was important to keep watch all night.

The son obeyed; but there was nothing to be seen but the countryside with its long shadows.

Then suddenly, a raven began to circle over the black mass of pines. There below, at the bottom of the valley where the river ran, you could see something like a whitish ribbon, glistening occasionally. It was no ribbon but a Moorish army, whose weapons threw off resplendent gleams in the moonlight.

Without any doubt, the prodigious host was headed for Pano, and had already entered the nearest next canyon. Oto got ready to spread the alarm, but his father held him back. He had a foreboding that he would perish in the imminent battle, and before that happened he wanted to tell Oto his last wishes.

They were these: that his son, if he survived the deadly skirmish, renounce the world, and, withdrawn to a cave on the mountain, dedicate the rest of his days in piety and prayer to God and to St. John the Baptist, to whom the father was very devoted. But if, at any time, he felt the vigor of his young blood drive him into the fight against the infidels, then he should abandon his sanctuary, go in search of his brothers in faith, gather them about him and establish a small army to start the reconquest of the invaded country.

Oto kissed his father. Tears streamed down his cheeks . . .

Immediately he went down to the settlement and sounded the alarm.

The leaders of the small garrison quickly exchanged what was on their minds. The old men, the women, and children were locked into the keep of the stronghold, and the men fit to do battle were allotted spots along the parapets and battlements, some to the towers, others to the gates . . .

The enemy army arrived at the foot of the walls. With savage cries, the Moors loosed their assault with more ferocity than courage. But there were so many of them, they had better weapons, and, after a desperate struggle, finished by sweeping over the heroic defenders.

The slaughter was horrible, frightful . . . The curved scimitars never tired of spilling blood. What a hideous night! The fierce assailants demolished the hovels and the fortress as well, among whose debris the population had perished . . . When the last moans of the last victims had been extinguished, the Muslims finally quit that field, filled as it was with anguish and death.

Dawn was coming . . . A very pale light was starting to redden the peaks . . . At the bottom of the fosse where the corpses were stacked up, a bloodstained body began to stir. It was Oto.

With great effort, he managed to stand erect on that havoc-ridden field, and, after coming to his senses, remembered that the Moors had flung him from the top of the wall; he felt bruised and had a wound across his forehead; but the cold of the night air had helped the blood coagulate.

As soon as he was able, he got to his feet and, reeling, he staggered about to find the bodies of his father and his brother. He found his father first. The old man was dead; but his pale forehead wore an expression of peace. Oto's eyes filled with tears, he prayed before the corpse of the beloved man, and later buried him at the same spot he'd taken his leave of him the night before.

Continuing the search among the lifeless bodies, he found

also his brother, who was still breathing. Oto hastened to take care of his wounds, which, happily, were not deep, and Félix was able to revive. When he found his feet, both brothers embraced with feeling, then little by little, they withdrew from the site of the slaughter.

Oto and Félix built a modest house, tilled the earth, and set themselves to hunting as well.

Oto added a letter to his name and called himself Voto, to remind himself to fulfill the promise he had made to his father. And a year passed . . .

It's a clear morning. Voto mounts a swift horse and is riding through the wood to hunt.

Suddenly, an enormous stag breaks from the thicket and sets out at a swift pace. Voto pursues him and spurs his horse on without pause. The creature and the knight pass through the forest and come out into an unbroken plain, one right behind the other . . . but neither notices that the ground cuts away sharply into a cliff . . . The stag flings himself headlong into the pass, very far down; the rider jerks the reins back, but it's already too late to hold the animal, and he dashes out over the void . . . Under the animal's hoofs no solid ground but a fathomless abyss . . .

Voto recommends himself to St. John the Baptist and steels himself for the deadly shock. But the horse hangs in the air miraculously. The rider hauls back on the rein; the charger twists and, again his hoofs rest on the lost meadow. After recovering from his terrible fright and having thanked God for the miracle, the horseman dismounts and peers over the edge of the precipice. The drop is covered with small bushes that dig into the rock for support . . . Voto climbs down a step at a time by the rough, steep indentation, no path at all . . . and finds a cave entrance, half-hidden by thorns and brambles.

Because the whole of that day's happenings had something of the mysterious about them—filled with dread, he enters the underground passage. At the back he catches a glimpse of a roughhewn altar cut into the rock, and on the altar a statue of St. John the Baptist lit by reflection off the back wall and the weak radiance of a wretchedly tiny lamp, whose light was constantly flickering out.

Rigid on the floor of the cavern stretched a corpse: the hermit. The old man's head rested against a triangular piece of stone upon which a few words had been scratched, which stated precisely that the old man's name was Juan, and that he had been born near the small town of Atarés.

This monk had built the rough altar, and had retired from this world to beg the Lord, through the mediation of John the Baptist, for the restoration of his country that'd been invaded so barbarously.

Voto knelt before the holy image and promised solemnly to retreat to such a life as the dead anchorite before him, to pray for the country in that same retirement, and for the remainder of his life.

Going home, he told Félix everything that had happened that memorable morning, and both brothers, leaving their clothing and all, dressed in coarse cloth, hid themselves away in the grotto, submitting themselves solely to penitence and to prayer.

They lived this way for fifteen long years, by the most austere discipline any monk might devise, with no incident whatever to disturb the solitude and peace of those wild altitudes.

Until one day they saw, outlined in the cave entrance, a man's silhouette. The new arrival took a few steps forward and collapsed . . .

The brothers ran over to him. He was badly wounded, having taken a terrible lance blow in the back. Félix and Voto hurried to catch him. They heard a short tale fall from his lips: the Moors had wounded him, and following his tracks and the trail of blood, had hounded him all the way up into these mountainous places where he was seeking ref-

uge, until, seeing him fall, they'd given him up for dead. It was not strictly true, however, and having discovered the opening to this cave, he had made a superhuman effort to reach it. But he had some good news to give them too: Pelayo, a Visigoth noble and friend of Roderico, had hoisted the colors of the True Faith, and in Christ's name, had just defeated the Moors in the far reaches of Asturias, near another grotto dedicated to Our Lady of Anseta, and which was called Covadonga.

Upon hearing these words, Voto remembered the counsels of his old father the night before he died.

"If someday you feel the vigor of your young blood drive you into the fight against the infidels, gather your brothers in religion and undertake the reconquest of our land . . ."

That day had arrived at last.

The next morning, still dressed as a monk, with a poor excuse for a walking stick in hand, Voto left to travel over the whole territory, hovel to hovel, village to village, from town to town . . . He was recruiting here and there the most determined and valiant men in all the mountains. To each one he summoned, he cited a day. On that particular day the man was to repair to the cave of San Juan Bautista.

As it happened . . . on the date determined, the most vigorous youngsters and the halest men of the Pyrenees headed for the cave at Atarés by every path and road in the mountains, putting their faith in God, but taking care not to be seen.

Not a single one missed the rendezvous at the hermitage, and there were over three hundred assembled. There they are in the cave, prostrated before the statue of San Juan Bautista, now raising their supplications to Our Lord God that He bless the enterprise they were about to undertake and guide their steps.

They elect from among their number, after that, the most

competent and devoted. Turns out, it is the valiant Garci
Ximénez, whom they proclaim king upon the spot.

This done, the assemblage of knights leave the cave at
Atarés to begin the reconquest of Aragón.

CATALUÑA

Two Legends of Count Vifredo

CHARLEMAGNE, THE EMPEROR with the flourishing beard, reigned in gentle France. Not much earlier than that, the bold Charles Martel had routed the Muslim troops at the famous battle of Poitiers; but the lord of Córdoba was keeping his eyes on the fruitful and fertile fields of ancient Gaul, and what was needed was to create a series of kingdoms and counties, both sides of the Pyrenees, and along their full breadth, to serve as a military barrier to the ambitions of the infidels.

In this way the kingdom of Aquitaine rose, and that of Navarre, which had first been a county, like those of Sobrarbe, Urgel, and some others, to all of which the French kings lent devoted support.

The county of Barcelona was governed by a nephew of the emperor, a certain Vifredo, to whom they had given the nickname, "the Hairy," inasmuch as he was extremely hirsute.

One day, Vifredo received a letter from Charlemagne, signed by his hand and sealed with his seal, wherein the emperor asked him to hasten to his aid in the war in which he was involved against the Normans.

Vifredo, valiant as a lion, spent no time in waiting. Off he went with his troops.

And Charles the Great of the flourishing beard and Vifredo

the Hairy attacked the enemy with such audacity that the
Normans were totally overcome. One of their archers, how-
ever, put an arrow through the chest of the valiant count of
Barcelona, who tumbled from his charger, bleeding heavily.

The news came to the emperor's ears, and he hurried immediately to the scene of the unhappy incident.

Vifredo had been carried off the battlefield and was
stretched out in a kingly tent in the encampment, when
Charlemagne himself appeared.

The count's intervention had been decisive, and the emperor wished to reward him generously, heaping him with
riches as recompense for an exploit so great as to be heroic,
though it was not the first, or even the second, in his series
of brilliant campaigns.

But Vifredo refused to accept any sort of booty for his
help, and asked only for some sign which would prove to the
world's eyes a recognition of his heroic services. What he de-
sired most was not riches or treasure, but an honor . . .

Charles noticed Vifredo's shield, whose golden field lacked
any figure or design to ennoble it. Then he wet the tips of
four fingers of his venerable hand in the blood flowing from
the open wound near Vifredo's heart, and setting them firmly
against the shield, drew, from top to bottom of the escutcheon
four bars, blood-red, which should thence be worn on his
arms, and which, from that time forward, has been prom-
inent on the coats-of-arms of all his descendants in the prince-
dom of Cataluña, and in the kingdoms of Aragón and Va-
lencia.

II

THE MOORS SPENT A DEAL OF TIME fighting the Christians, but
as it happened, the county of Cataluña refused to fall into
their hands. It became necessary to resort to a new weapon,
one that would sow panic in the enemy camp. And some

prompt-witted Moor, we don't know who he was, came up with the cheerful idea to import a dragon, a fearful dragon, into Cataluña.

These kinds of monsters existed at that time in Africa. The Moors trapped a small one there, a small young one, but already he flew like an eagle and ran like a bull. They brought the little monster into the deep valley of Llobregat and set him in one of the many caves that burrow into the Mountain of San Lloréns. They left him there, certain that when he was grown and become adult, he would contribute decisively to the overthrow of the Catalans.

The dragon, in reality, was still nursing, and the Moors had to take care of his feeding until he was fully developed. It was much to their interest that the monster attain great size and ferocity, and he had to be raised correctly. Therefore, they brought him ewes, baby calves, and whatever other animals they carried off from the Christians in their frequent raids. The baby dragon gobbled up this fare like a child takes to the bottle, until he could get along by himself. And then! What satisfaction the Moors took, for the fierce beast they had raised in the caverns of San Lloréns was the most ferocious that had ever been heard of. Naturally, nothing comparable had ever existed in Spain. In a single day he was devouring whole flocks, and if he didn't find them, or was still hungry, he ate people also.

The whole of Cataluña lived in constant terror, and in the valley of the Llobregat mere existence proved impossible. Everyone was wailing, and the good count Vifredo wanted to put an end to this terrible calamity.

He summoned then his most renowned warrior, Sir Spes (whose name, in Latin, means hope), and put under his command a troop of men selected from among the best in the whole Catalan army, and at their head he was to seek out the monster and either capture or kill him.

The knight, Sir Spes, and his war-toughened veterans rode off at a gallop, reins loose, with fretted visors and pikes in

their lance rests, determined to kill the dragon or die in the engagement.

When the riders reached the monster's cave, a little tired from the road which was mostly uphill, the dragon was engorging a man. But seeing his assailants, he loosed his prey, a swift run and he took to the air to attack them, all with a frightful hissing and a bellowing that raised the hair on their heads.

Vifredo's soldiers felt their blood freeze; but overpowering their justifiable terror and determined to die in the attempt, they set spurs to their chargers. But the frightened horses reared, swung about, and set out on a crazy, breathless run which the riders could not check, even up to when, frothing and sweated, they leaped headlong into a chasm, at the bottom of which all the animals and many of the men perished. That spot with its terrible glory is still called the Knights' Abyss.

When the survivors returned and entered the presence of the valiant count, they were still shaking.

Listening to their story, Vifredo felt his blood boil, and ordering his arms and his horse, he set out for the Mountain of San Lloréns completely alone. But on the road he cut off the branch of a tree, a good thick one. And thus he presented himself in front of the cave, which gave off a fetid and asphyxiating smell.

The dragon was inside. Vifredo came closer to the cave entrance and began to shove the branch into it until it fetched up against the scaly skin of the dragon. There was a fierce howl, and he split the branch with one thud of a claw, but in such a way that one of the hunks fell across the other, forming a cross.

The count took this fortuitous accident as a sign from heaven and, filled with courage, he unsheathed his sword and hurled himself toward the dragon to kill or be killed.

But the weapon no more than scratched the monster's skin; he seized the count in his enormous claws and got ready to fly, stretching his enormous, robust bat-wings incredibly wide.

The count's efforts were useless. There was no way to disengage himself. And the dragon sailed off into the air, Vifredo still in his claws, with the pieces of tree branches still in the shape of a cross.

The count fixed his eyes upon the cross, recommending his soul to God with all his heart. He kept jabbing from beneath with his lance, which he had not lost, despite the heat of the combat. He guessed where the monster's heart was located, and with a well-aimed thrust, split it in a single blow.

The dragon was dead; but he did not fall immediately but much farther on, upon the mountain that's still called Cerro de la Cruz, Cross Ridge.

Miraculously, the count of Barcelona came out of it unharmed. With his inflexible boldness, he ended by saving the country from the most terrible of scourges.

The dragon's skin, stuffed with straw, was put on exhibition in Barcelona, so that the whole world might admire the bravery of Vifredo the Hairy.

St. Martin's Sword

"Sir," said the lookout, "a Moorish army is coming, coming up through Bañolas to the plains of Santa Pau."

The count of Besalú commanded his courser on the double, ordered that the trumpets blow the alarm, and that the soldiers repair to the castle's courtyard. All of them gathered there, and there they split up the army so as to confront the enemy.

The count of Besalú was a thunderbolt in war, had won a well-merited reputation, and was numbered as one of the most valiant champions of Christendom.

He launched the attack against the infidels at the head of his men with the impetus of a rock torn off and rolling downgrade. At the first clash, he demolished a Moor built like a castle, threaded a second on his lance, smashed down a third, and setting hand to his sharp-biting sword, split a fourth enemy down to the gut, cleaving him from the crest of his helmet down to the saddle. He swung immediately against another attacker and stretched him on the ground with another powerful chop; but this time the sword leapt from his hand and broke into smithereens.

In the clamor of the combat, the count found himself unarmed, and with no other choice than to get out of there, rather than die uselessly.

The fray arrived at its critical point, and the encounter was not decisive on either side.

The count of Besalú, however, was not only a warrior, he was also a good Christian, and thought that if his strong arm were already powerless to aid his people, at least his deep-rooted faith might assist them further. He headed his horse, all sweated up, toward a shrine near the battlefield, dedicated, as it happened, to San Martín. The count leapt agilely from the saddle and entered the darkened sanctuary, knelt before the altar. His prayer was desperate and fervent:

"Sir, milord, San Martín, O firm believer and good knight: do not abandon my men in the fray: aid them, though I lack a weapon to return to battle against the enemies of Christ and your Holy Church . . .

While the count was eagerly praying, the brave Catalans noted his absence and started to retreat, demoralized by the loss of so great a leader.

Meanwhile, the count had knelt there, engrossed in his praying, and perhaps for that reason, a dream came to him that he could actually see: the saint's statue began to move, he moved his right hand to his belt, ungirt his sword, and handed it to the ardent count, close enough for him to seize it. The count of Besalú rubbed his eyes. Was he still dreaming? But San Martín continued the gesture, offering him his sword.

And the count wavered no longer; he stretched out his arm and gripped the weapon, got to his feet and left the shrine quickly, mounted his charger in a single leap, dug in his spurs again and headed back toward the battlefield.

The count of Besalú opened a passage between his men like a waterspout, until he'd set himself at their head.

"SAN MARTÍN!" he cried in a stentorian voice, attacking the mass of Moors violently.

In a short time, Saracen corpses completely covered the Plain of Santa Fe. The Catalans' victory had been complete and absolute.

The victors were returning then to Besalú, when battle fatigue obliged them to make a halt at Collsatrapa.

Up to that point, the soldiers had spoken very little among themselves; besides, during the brief tranquillity of a rest in such a fair place, the moment seemed right for each of them to discuss the details of the encounter. And all agreed that never had they seen their lord lay on such dreadful strokes, despite the fact they had fought with him in numerous battles. But on this occasion, it seemed as though his sword had grown manifold, laying out the edge of the sword with strokes more deadly cutting than any they had ever seen.

The count was listening to these comments, and was not even slightly embarrassed to relate the happenstance: San Martín had given him his sword. But the explanation was so incredible that the soldiers started to smile . . .

Then the count unsheathed the miraculous weapon, and flourishing it with incomparable skill, he let it fall upon an enormous boulder and clove it in half.

The stone still exists and is called Pedratallada, the Cleft Rock. But there are very few left who know and can relate that it was the count of Besalú who split it, using the sword of San Martín.

VALENCIA

The Maiden's Staircase

ON THE OLD ROAD between Almansa and Játiva, full in the center of the Valencian plain, the town of Mogente stands, as it happens, split in two parts by the Bosquet River, a tributary of the Albaida, which, in turn, flows into the Júcar.

The Bosquet and the road run together through a valley flanked by two massive bulks of mountains on the spurs of the Sierra Énguera.

Just beyond that, lifted on a promontory of sharp rocks that seems to have been piled together by a legendary hand, rises Montesa Castle, well-known from the military order from which it took its name.

Orchards of carob trees and oranges grace the brilliant and fertile landscape, whose system of development and irrigation dates from Moorish times. On one of the mountains that impinge on the river, just at the entrance of the village, there is a staircase of very high and unequal steps, known by the people who live there as Escala de la Doncella, the Maiden's Staircase. This particular stair has a very ancient history, had, even in Moorish times, back to when the wise, valorous, and prudent Sidi Mohammed Ben Abderramán Ben Tahir was lord of Mogente and of its fortress, now long fallen into ruins.

Ben Tahir was a very cultivated man; he had a deep affection for literature, wrote poems himself, took great satisfaction both in books and in his rugged, provincial life, and devoted himself to it during those scarce times of pleasure which his obligations as governor and warrior afforded him.

But the object of his greatest affection and care, of his most subtle fears and his most affectionate watchfulness, was a daughter, educated with the greatest nicety by a sage old man who had been captured by the Almohades, and whose ransom had cost Ben Tahir close to a fortune.

The daughter was called Flor de los Jardines, Flower of the Gardens, let's call her Flora, for short. And she really seemed so, because she was good, intelligent, and very pretty. Also, she loved nature, and Ben Tahir had built the maiden a tower which connected to the fortress by a long corridor, and which overlooked a great stretch of countryside.

At the same time as he was reading her lessons in geography, history, and religion, the scholar and ex-captive taught Flora the art or science of magic.

With such wide knowledge and of such a lovely appearance, it's no wonder that Flor de los Jardines found such great favor among knights of her own age.

But, in spite of the fact that her father's solicitude and the attentions of her numerous suitors always saw to it that her slightest caprice was fulfilled, Ben Tahir's daughter was a melancholy woman, a dreamer, sad and set in her own ways.

Her father resolved to divert her, and thought that nothing would be more to the purpose than to take her with him on a trip.

And both of them set out on the road; together they visited the most magnificent courts of Al-Andalus, where the mere presence of Flora raised a whole storm of love. Between the princes and the wealthiest knights with the greatest patrimony and the most sparkling prospects, she had more suitors than you could count on the fingers of both hands. But the young woman rejected them all, wishing only to return to her solitary tower, its murmuring rivulet nearby, to there amuse herself, completely abstracted, absorbed in her long meditations.

As Ben Tahir noticed that his daughter's teacher also passed long hours sunk into an equal abstraction and a like sadness, one fine day he demanded that he confess to him the reason for such a state of mind. The old scholar, astrologer, and wizard, spoke in this wise:

"Allah keep you, O noble Ben Tahir! You ask me the reasons for our sadnesses, and I must tell you that they arise from very diverse reasons. Your daughter is depressed because it is needful to fill her soul with love, as with any young lady; but she's so delicate and so intelligent, she masters the arts and sciences so well . . . in a word, she is so superior to the people who surround her, that she can maintain no hopeful anticipation from any one of them, since she knows more of the sciences than the scholars, and further, she knows herself more powerful than princes. Your daughter's ideal does not exist in the world, and nonetheless, she has not resigned herself to live without him. Where my case is concerned, the reason's very different: I feel my age more every day; I realize that my existence will stop any day now and quickly, and I would like to go home, that my days might end themselves in the same country where I was born."

Ben Tahir found himself very perplexed and did not wish to grant the old man the permission he'd asked for without consulting first with Flor de los Jardines, whose health, naturally, was a much greater concern to him.

He went, then, to speak with his daughter, and explained to her what the old man had claimed.

Flora answered: "My father: in no way do I want my maestro to leave until he teaches me the last and greatest of the several secrets he possesses, a secret which, up until now, he has not wanted to reveal to me. As soon as he tells it to me, I shall be completely happy."

The intractable Ben Tahir required that the old maestro come immediately into his presence, and there told him about the conversation he had just had with Flora, and the answer she had given him. In which case, the desires of the scholar

and of the young girl could be assuaged jointly, given that the old man would reveal his secret to her . . .

The ancient captive listened to his lord attentively and then said:

"Flora's wish includes a very serious danger. Your daughter has discovered that the gigantic staircase cut into those nearby rocks leads to an enchanted palace, filled with wonders and dazzling opulence; the ascent by such high steps is impossible, for they were not made for mortal beings, for such poor creatures as ourselves. Consequently, it would be unrealizable to get into that celebrated palace, if there were no other means to enter it."

"And this other means exists?"

"It exists, yes, and I know it. That precisely is my secret. But I have struggled against revealing it to her because the risk, to which I have just referred, demands much too much preparation to deal with it."

"So, it is imperative that my daughter know your secret; and if you refuse to reveal it, I'll throw you into jail for the rest of your life, or maybe I'll just get rid of you . . . In any case, the decision is yours," threatened Ben Tahir.

"My decision is at your pleasure. But I warn you that the entrance I know is so dangerous that your daughter might remain in the palace enchanted, over the whole of eternity."

"In that case, I shall myself accompany Flor de los Jardines, and you will come with us also; understood, of course, that my servants will receive orders to cut off your head, if it happens that my daughter and I happen to remain in this marvelous fortress, and you manage to save only yourself."

"As you like, milord. I shall be waiting for you at the first cockcrow on the mysterious stairs."

It was midnight when Ben Tahir and Flor de los Jardines, exacting in their rendezvous, arrived at the foot of the staircase. The old magician was already there. He lit a lantern to illuminate the worn pages of a very ancient book.

He read in a high voice, and when he had finished the first page, a terrifying rumble was heard from underground.

The old man continued his reading impassively; the rumble grew stronger still, and, upon finishing the second page, a great crevice suddenly opened in the mountainside.

Ben Tahir and Flora were filled with dread; they had lost almost any power of movement; it paralyzed them with terror.

The magician kept on reading until he'd finished the third page, meanwhile the enormous cleft continued growing wider every moment. The walls of rock were being split by a magic power, little by little . . . Inside, a magnificent palace could be seen . . . Glittering lights illumined the most fabulous treasures that could be imagined. The gilded roofs were held up by emerald columns and the high walls were studded with precious stones.

The old man drew out a pipe, blew upon it, and Flora and Ben Tahir, stunned from contemplating such a wonder, were hurried into the inside of a marvelous enclosure.

While father and daughter walked timidly up and down through the enchanted fortress, the scholar continued reading, without ceasing, those words, incomprehensible to them.

An hour passed. The magician began to whistle again on his pipe, and Ben Tahir and Flor de los Jardines ran to the exit. Once they were outside the mountain, the rocks closed behind them, roaring and shuddering like an erupting volcano.

The lord of Mogente and the lady radiated happiness, though keeping the marvels they had seen absolutely secret from everyone, and the former granted permission to the magician, as he so wanted, to return to his home, but under the condition that he deliver to Flora the magic book. Which the ancient maestro did, and Ben Tahir and his daughter remained in possession of it.

And years passed. Ben Tahir and Flor de los Jardines were

fortunate in possessing such an incantation which would open the charmed fortress.

But then a day came when the lord of Mogente found his daughter missing. He ordered his many servants to search the palace, and no one could find her. Under proper interrogations, her slaves revealed that she had been seen leaving at midnight with one servant only, whom she had ordered to wait for her at the foot of the gigantic stair; but hours and hours had passed, and Flor de los Jardines had not yet returned.

Ben Tahir needed no further explanation; he raced like a madman to the stairs and began desperately to call to his daughter. From within the earth was heard a pitiful moan . . . then another. It was Flora's voice.

The father, helpless when it came to disenchanting the daughter he loved so dearly, ordered all his slaves and servants to start to demolish the damnable staircase and to raze the mountain. But as the diggings grew deeper with the exhausting work and exhausted forces, the maiden's voice was heard proportionately weaker. The moans, nonetheless, incited them to continue until they dropped, dog-tired, one after another, weakened by efforts as superhuman as they were useless.

Ben Tahir understood finally that only magic could break this spell, and took ship to Africa to visit the scholar-magician, who lived in Mequinez, to see if he could resolve it and put an end to this intolerable waiting.

But when Ben Tahir finally found the old magician's house, he found him prostrate on his couch and at the point of death. Nevertheless, he steeled himself and attempted to be gracious; but in answer to the anguished questions of her aggrieved father, he could barely reply, stutteringly, that his magic science was insufficient to disenchant Flor de los Jardines. And so saying, he died.

Desperate and worn out with grief, Ben Tahir died of sorrow the next day . . .

Now and again, the old men of the village say, the girl's wailing and lamentation are still heard, especially when the hour draws toward midnight.

For hundreds and hundreds of years, there has come an incredible apparition, which the oldest men in Mogente re-affirm on their strongest oaths, and even the inhabitants of nearby villages: a very beautiful woman, decked out in the most brilliant jewels and finery, more like a houri inhabiting the Muslim paradise than any human being, descends the staircase in a majestic fashion, and waits for a simple mortal to approach her one day with the intent of disenchanting her. But the truth is that, for six centuries now, no one has been able to do that, despite the fact that any man who could suc-ceed at that could be married to such an excellently lovely maiden . . .

Perhaps it is only a vain longing, and that it's true, the daughter of Ben Tahir must remain enchanted for all eternity.

MURCIA

The Phantom
Ship

DON FELIPE III OF HAPSBURG was ruling Spain when the so-called "regimental curtain" was raised in Murcia. This was the name given to a palisade separating the two camps in which were the lists, or enclosures where the chivalrous sports of that time were to be performed: tournaments, jousts, races, jousting with reed spears, and other activities. And "to raise the curtain" meant the same as to organize the before-mentioned fiestas. In them, knights from all over the country had a chance to try their expertise.

One of those who shone most to advantage in the then-renowned jousts and tournaments of Cartagena was a young man from Cáceres, Don Luis de Garre, for his carriage, for his arrogance, for his valor, and for his nimbleness. A long somber involvement had estranged him from the city for two years, at the end of which he returned full of pride and hopes for resuming his life of triumphs on the field and in the tourneys, and also in the field of amorous conquests, for he was a handsome and spirited youth.

Unluckily, the condition of his ethics did not match his physical appearance.

Before his voluntary exile from Cartagena, he had addressed his attentions to a lovely young lady of whom he was enamored to the point of madness: I am referring to Doña

Leonor de Ojeda, daughter of the governor of the castle in which she lived with her father.

The knight, Don Luis, loved Doña Leonor passionately; but the governor's daughter was engaged to Don Carlos de Laredo, a young man of excellent reputation, who returned her affection with a deep tenderness.

Don Luis' aspirations, therefore, had not the slightest possibility of being fulfilled. Don Carlos and Doña Leonor were very much in love, and her gallant possessed all the same qualities as Don Luis, and in addition had the favor of his betrothed.

The despair of the knight from Garre and his jealousy of another's happiness, led him to commit the worst of injustices.

He guessed that Don Carlos' life cloaked a tragic secret, and he availed himself of certain informations to revenge himself upon the knight and to destroy his happiness.

It was during the years when religious intolerance dominated the countries of the world. Spain was carrying on a bloody battle throughout Europe against the Protestant princes, and in the Mediterranean against Turkish and Algerian pirates.

The kings feared that these latter might be in contact with the Moriscos and the Jews in the interior of the peninsula, and, under the impression that they were masters of others' consciences as much as they were of their own possessions, they had driven both these peoples out of the country, under pain of death.

The tribunal of the Holy Office of the Inquisition spied unceasingly on supposed heretics, and once they were convicted and had confessed to holding a religion other than Catholic, they were delivered over to His Majesty's justice for punishment. In the most severe cases, the punishment was death, in the worst cases of apostasy and stubbornness, i.e., contempt of court.

In such a society so obsessed by the Faith and so contemptful toward charity, priests, and nuns, and those who were not either were induced, in God's service, to commit crimes that resembled one another closely.

For this reason, then, those who professed a religion different from the ruling religion of the country or from that practiced by its prince, lived in jeopardy, risking the hardiest dangers, inside or outside of Spain. And this happened to be the case with Don Carlos de Laredo, a name and title which concealed under it Yusuf Ben Ali, son of Mohammed and brother of Fátima, all of them reputable and devoted Muslims, but concealed behind a seeming Catholicism in which they did not believe at all.

It is never good to affect one religion and to practice another: deceit merits the most explicit reprimand; but the fault in this case might be extenuated by a very real fear of death, besides which, Mohammed and his sons were entirely persuaded that in professing the Muslim faith, they were serving God.

The depraved Don Luis had to do very little to get rid of his favored rival; simply denounce him as a concealed Morisco.

The Holy Office of the Inquisition seized Yusuf Ben Ali, who was condemned to the ultimate penalty. His faith and his courage were good companions to the end, and he died in the bonfire at the stake, commending himself to God and proclaiming his firm belief in the religion of Mohammed.

Doña Leonor de Ojeda, entirely dismayed, rejected the knightly informer with loathing; the unhappy father, Mohammed, fell seriously sick of a profound sadness and melancholy; he found consolation only in Fátima, the deeply affectionate sister, who detailed to him her plans that this hair-raising murder of her brother should not go unpunished.

Aside from simply being vicious, Don Luis was furthermore a coward, and disappeared from Spain.

Feeling himself at the point of death, Mohammed made Fátima swear that she would avenge her brother's death, and then delivered up his spirit.

Finally, after two years, the story appeared to have been forgotten. New incidents attracted people's attention, and Don Luis returned to Cartagena to show himself off splendidly within the palisades of the recently lifted "curtain."

Handsome women fought among themselves over him, and the knight was constantly receiving notes more or less expressing a love which he was used to inspiring.

One day, someone managed to arrange that a letter reach the knight's hands, and it went like this:

". . . if, in protecting a lady, you be as courageous as you were this afternoon on the 'Field of the Curtain,' when curfew tolls I shall wait for you in the ruined mill at the top of the Canteras road."

Don Luis did not think it had anything to do with danger; he imagined that the note concealed a plea for a love rendezvous, since the handwriting was that of a woman and he was quite accustomed to such incidents. So, then, at the appointed hour, he showed up at the mill. It was totally dark by that time.

And, in fact, a few minutes later he heard the footsteps of a young woman, who was not slow to present herself, her face hidden by her cloak, as was the custom among ladies of that period and rather daring in style.

The lady's words disclosed interest first, then inclination. Don Luis allowed himself to be very taken by the veiled woman, very flattered indeed, because she seemed to be a rich and important lady if you judged by her conversation and her clothes. The quality of her hands and shape were those of a beautiful woman.

It was hot . . . The lady offered Don Luis a refreshing drink; the knight drained the cup . . . The conversation continued, becoming more and more interesting, and all at once, Don Luis collapsed onto the floor.

The lady then took out some ropes which she had hidden under her clothing and lashed together the hands and feet of the man on the floor.

Then she emerged from the ruined mill, made a signal, and two men appeared with a litter. They rolled the unconscious knight onto it and started off. The veiled lady was right behind them.

They walked in the moonlight along the edge of the lower slopes of Sicilia Mountain, today called Atalaya, and finally stopped at a small inlet near an ancient Muslim hermitage or sanctuary called Selin El Algamek.

From this early Moorish name, the cove in our day called Algameca was derived.

A skiff appeared on the sea and approached the beach rapidly; then the lady and the still-unconscious knight disappeared into the small boat.

The light craft rowed out until it came alongside a galley which hoisted colors bearing a half-moon.

When the prisoner began to recover his senses, he found himself on the lowest deck of the vessel under full sail headed for Algiers. Beside him, the veiled lady held a vial of salts to his nostrils, no doubt the same that had brought him to again.

Don Luis wanted to rise, but could not; the stiff cords prevented him from budging. But his consternation and terror subsided to the point where he could now recognize, in the veiled lady of the evening before, the features of the unfortunate Yusuf's sister, Fátima.

For an instant, the knight's mind was filled with the passage of a horrible vision, that of the young Don Carlos, withering, burned in the crackling bonfire, through his fault.

Fátima did not leave him time to meditate; he was forced to hear from her lips his terrible sentence: he would not be sacrificed immediately, like her unhappy brother; he was condemned to the fearful life of a galley slave, rowing galleons as a prisoner, fastened to the benches of ships with heavy chains, taking continually the whiplashes of the ship's master on his shoulders every time he slacked off, or failed to put forward an enormous effort to drive the ship . . . And this for his whole life, without hope of ransom. This was worse than death. Yusuf and Mohammed had been avenged.

For an instant the light penetrated the dark enclosure, and the figure of Fátima leaving filled the hatch. Then the half-door closed, and the shadows spread back into every corner.

It was necessary to escape or to die trying.

Nipping with his teeth, pulling with superhuman efforts, Don Luis succeeded in loosening the bonds from his wrists; then both feet and, at random then, he began groping about for an extinguished lantern which was hanging from the ceiling and which he had accidentally seen in the brief seconds that the hatchway had been open.

When he had the lantern in his hands, he got from his pouch a flint and steel and some straw, intending to light it, and in fact he made fire . . . But then the ship heaved as it struck a wave heavily which flung him against the low bench. He instantly regained his feet, but the burning straw had landed on a pile of burlap and lines covered with pitch, out of which blazed a terrifying flash of fire. A heavy, thick, black smoke filled the hold and was choking the prisoner. Painfully, Don Luis began to seek some way out, looking on the scene, terrified, as the fire was reaching now a cask of gunpowder. But he felt his strength leaving him. He, too, was about to die in another holocaust. There was no doubt but that it was a punishment from heaven.

He hunkered down on his knees and begged God to pardon him his many sins; but, above all for the crime he had committed against the innocent Yusuf.

A hair-raising explosion, followed by many others, resounded out over the spacious sea. Thick cloud enveloped the remains of the burning ship, and a few seconds later, it was swallowed by the waters.

Fishermen out of La Azohia, Porús, Escombreras and other ports along that coast, know that on the Day of the Virgin every year, just at dawn, an explosion is heard on the sea, something like a cannon shot, and after a few brief seconds,

the silhouette of a mysterious vessel issues from the waters of the sea and floats upon it, like a shadow, and afterward vanishes.

They've given it the name, the *Phantom Ship*.

ANDALUCÍA

The Old Woman
of the Candilejo

IN SEVILLA, there is a street called the Candilejo, which is the name for a small kitchen lamp. This name evokes an event from the time of Pedro I of Castile, whose followers called him *the Just*, and whose enemies called him *the Cruel*.

It was Don Pedro's great pleasure to live in Sevilla; he had its Moorish fortress restored, enlarged it with magnificent salons, and passed long seasons there. Still today, after centuries have passed, an ancient and twisted orange tree is preserved in its wonderful gardens, which, according to tradition, was planted by the same Don Pedro.

It was a lugubrious, murky night. Not a sound could be heard in the narrow lane whose citizens were already asleep, no doubt, but for the little old woman who lived alone in a wretched house . . .

Suddenly, the clash of swords was heard, right there, at the corner where the street turned, and shortly afterward, an agonized voice crying out: *"God protect me! I'm dying!"*

The little old lady, without considering the consequences such an act might have, caught up the small kitchen lamp and hurried over to a crude and tiny window in the house. By the weak, flickering light of the lamp, she could see then the bulky figure of a man bathed in blood, fallen upon the cobblestones of the street, and, beside him, a robust knight, very tall, who remained there with the sword in his right hand.

The lamplight illumined the face of the killer, who hastened to cover it with both hands, so that the curious woman could not recognize him later.

Perhaps regretting what she had just done, the old woman hastily withdrew from the window; but by ill luck or perhaps through awkwardness, the small lamp fell into the street.

Her curiosity had not been satisfied; she still stood behind the blinds to listen, and soon she heard the murderer's footsteps down by the wall, and the sound which she already recognized very well, that of his kneecaps creaking when he walked.

By this extraordinary noise, she knew that the murderer was also a knight who, at the same time each night, walked under her window. The old woman had glanced at him furtively, seen him more than once, and knew who he was.

"Lord save us, Virgin of the Three Kings!" she exclaimed, and began to recite her prayers.

The following morning, the city constables came across the victim's corpse, and the lord mayor, who was Don Martín Fernández Cerón, swiftly instituted his inquiries in order to uncover and jail the assassin.

Jews and Moriscos, who lived in the neighborhood, were under suspicion. Someone mentioned a beautiful lady who received some important personage in the early hours of the morning; but no one knew who the lover might be.

The neighbors nearest to the scene of the crime knew absolutely nothing, nor had heard anything, nor had anything to declare.

The occurrence raised a good deal of comment in Sevilla, and no slight censure of the authorities for their negligence. Finally, the public rumbling came to the ears of the king himself, like a sea-swell of protests against his courts of justice, a name given generically to those entrusted to execute it.

Don Pedro had to step into the matter, and hastily sent for the lord mayor.

"Is it possible that a man has been murdered inside Sevilla, and neither you nor your constables have yet found out who is guilty of it? Have you not even found a clue that would serve you as a trail which would lead you to him? Can you exercise that way the justice which has given me my good name?"

The lord mayor made excuses for himself in vain:

"Milord, we have completed all imaginable investigations; but I must admit that, so far, the results have been useless. The only item we found on the site was a lantern knocked up against the wall of a house where a poor woman, a very little old lady, lives. Doubtless it belongs to her. But what can we prove with that?"

"Have you taken testimony from this elderly woman?"

"Yes, your Highness; and she recognized the lamp as hers; but she assures us that she knows nothing else."

"Seize her again and bring her into my presence. I assure you that in front of me she will have to make a deposition."

The lord mayor left the royal fortress in a hurry and very frightened. He knew very well that if the king's attention was attracted by the case and if it were not cleared up quickly, it would be his head would have to pay for the mysterious killer, and he was already minutes behind in accomplishing the orders as given.

Several hours later, Don Martín returned to the castle and the following scene took place in one of its Moorish halls:

"Milord, this is the old woman," said Don Martín.

The fragile woman was trembling with fear. When could she ever have imagined herself before the king, in a palace that seemed to her like a legend? No contrast could have been more speaking than this, that wrinkled and stooped old woman, twisted like a bundle of vine shoots, small, abject, almost exhausted and the corpulent monarch with the hard visage, a cold glance, in the flower of his youth and surrounded with an oriental luxury.

The lord mayor asked: "Do you recognize this lamp?"

"Yes . . . I have told you already that it's mine," stammered the old woman.

"And you did not recognize the person who killed the knight?"

"I didn't see . . ."

"All right, that's fine," the mayor continued. "You want us to compel you to confess and you're going to do so very quickly."

The fat, ugly executioners seized their pizzles and were ready to whip them savagely against the slight old lady, when the monarch spoke:

"If you know who the killer is, I order that you declare his name. My justice is the same for everyone, and no one need fear it."

But the old woman, pallid and quaking, was not bold enough to look Don Pedro in the eye; he must have seemed to her some kind of demigod.

All she could manage was to stammer several unintelligible words.

"Begin . . ." Don Martín ordered the executioners.

"Not yet," said Don Pedro. "Woman, for the last time, I command that you denounce the assassin, whoever he might be, and if you do not do so I shall send you to the gallows."

"Answer!" shouted the mayor, beside himself. "Let's have it now . . . Who was it?"

But the old woman kept her mouth closed. Don Pedro insisted once more, Don Martín went back to threatening, the executioners approached the victim and she found that so menacing that, finally, drawing some resolution forth from her feebleness, she answered timidly but with self-possession:

"The king."

Terror paralysed the executioners' arms and sealed Don Martín's mouth. Sweet heaven, what was going to happen? Better the earth open and swallow them all before the dreaded sovereign open his mouth.

But Don Pedro, in a firm and temperate voice, broke

that deathly silence by declaring to the general astonishment: "You have spoken the truth and justice will protect you."

Then he drew out a purse containing a hundred pieces of gold and handed it to the woman, adding: "Take it: the king, Don Pedro knows how to reward whoever serves him well."

The old lady thought she must be dreaming, meanwhile she took the bag . . .

The monarch continued . . .

"As far as the murderer is concerned, he shall be executed . . . You hear that, Don Martín . . ."

The mayor began to shake; chills spread over his whole body, from his toenails to the tips of his venerable hair.

Once more the voice of Don Pedro, serious, quiet, drew him from his anguished uncertainty. The sovereign continued:

"However, as no one can execute the king of Castile, I order that his effigy be decapitated, that its head be cut off and that the same be placed on the same corner of the street where the knight was killed, so that it serve as a caution to all the people."

And so it was done. For many years afterward, a head of Don Pedro the Cruel was nailed up on that corner of the street of the Candilejo.

The Author

ANTONIO JIMÉNEZ-LANDI is a distinguished Spanish poet and author of many successful adult and juvenile books. Born in Madrid in 1909, he received his degree in philosophy and literature from the University of Madrid. He lives in Madrid, where he divides his time between writing and working as a children's book consultant for a large publishing house.

The Translator

PAUL BLACKBURN, one of America's most gifted poets and translators, was educated at the University of Wisconsin and the University of Toulouse in France. He was born in St. Albans, Vermont, in 1926 and died in New York in 1971. In addition to his own books of poetry, such as *The Dissolving Fabric, The Cities, Three Dreams and an Old Poem,* and *The Nets,* he translated the works of Julio Cortázar, Octavio Paz, Federico García Lorca, and Pablo Picasso.

DATE DUE

30 505 JOSTEN'S